THE PUBLICATIONS COMMITEE OF THE COUNCIL

Twentyfirst annual report of the Council of Missions

Cooperating with the Church of Christ in Japan

THE PUBLICATIONS COMMITEE OF THE COUNCIL

Twentyfirst annual report of the Council of Missions
Cooperating with the Church of Christ in Japan

ISBN/EAN: 9783741169205

Manufactured in Europe, USA, Canada, Australia, Japa

Cover: Foto ©Andreas Hilbeck / pixelio.de

Manufactured and distributed by brebook publishing software
(www.brebook.com)

THE PUBLICATIONS COMMITEE OF THE COUNCIL

Twentyfirst annual report of the Council of Missions

Cooperating with the Church of Christ in Japan

THE PUBLICATIONS COMMITEE OF THE COUNCIL

Twentyfirst annual report of the Council of Missions
Cooperating with the Church of Christ in Japan

ISBN/EAN: 9783741169205

Manufactured in Europe, USA, Canada, Australia, Japa

Cover: Foto ©Andreas Hilbeck / pixelio.de

Manufactured and distributed by brebook publishing software
(www.brebook.com)

THE PUBLICATIONS COMMITEE OF THE COUNCIL

Twentyfirst annual report of the Council of Missions

TWENTY-FIRST
NNUAL REPORT OF THE COUNCIL
OF MISSIONS

CO OPERATING WITH THE

CHURCH OF CHRIST IN JAPAN.

ISSUED BY THE PUBLICATIONS COMMITTEE

OF THE COUNCIL.

1 8 9 8.

OFFICERS OF THE COUNCIL
FOR 1898-99.

RESIDENT - - - - - - H. B. PRICE.
ICE PRESIDENT - - - - J. B. HAIL.
ECRETARY - - - - - - ALBERT OLTMANS.
REASURER - - - - - - JOHN C. BALLAGH.

PUBLICATIONS COMMITTEE.

WILLIAM IMBRIE.

E. ROTHESAY MILLER.

M. N. WYCKOFF.

H. B. PRICE.

T. M. MacNAIR.

H. M. LANDIS.

S. S. SNYDER.

3

CONTENTS.

5

5. REPORTS OF STANDING COMMITTEES AND TREASURER :

   1. Publications.
   2. Statistics.
   3. Self-support.
   4. Sunday School Literature.
   5. Finances of Council.

6. REPORTS OF SPECIAL COMMITTEES APPOINTED BY THIS COUNCIL :

   1. Teaching of the Scriptures and the Creed of the Church.
   2. General Missionary Conference of Evangelical Missions in Japan.
   3. Resolutions regarding Dr. Verbeck.

7. MISCELLANEOUS RESOLUTIONS :

   1. Commentaries on the Scriptures and Tract on Baptism.
   2. Systematic giving.
   3. Special day of prayer.
   4. Treaty revision and Christianity.
   5. Education of the children of missionaries in Japan.
   6. Barrows Lectureship.
   7. Opening sermon of the President.
   8. General report of the work of next year.
   9. Next annual meeting of the Council.
   10. Entertainment Committee.

11. Officers and Publications Committee for next year.

IV. OUTLINE OF ADDRESSES DELIVERED AT THE MEMORIAL SERVICE.

V. ROLL OF THE COUNCIL:

1. EAST JAPAN MISSION OF THE PRESBYTERIAN CHURCH IN THE U. S. A. (Northern).
2. WEST JAPAN MISSION OF THE PRESBYTERIAN CHURCH IN THE U. S. A. (Northern).
3. NORTH JAPAN MISSION OF THE REFORMED (Dutch) CHURCH IN AMERICA.
4. SOUTH JAPAN MISSION OF THE REFORMED (Dutch) CHURCH IN AMERICA.
5. MISSION OF THE UNITED PRESBYTERIAN CHURCH OF SCOTLAND.
6. MISSION OF THE PRESBYTERIAN CHURCH IN THE U. S. (Southern).
7. MISSION OF THE REFORMED (German) CHURCH IN THE U. S.
8. MISSION OF THE CUMBERLAND PRESBYTERIAN CHURCH.
9. WOMANS UNION MISSIONARY SOCIETY.

GENERAL REPORT OF THE WORK OF THE YEAR

BY THE

Rev. H. K. MILLER.

———

Provision having been made for separate reports from the Committees on Publications, Statistics, Self-support, and Sunday School Lesson Helps, these subjects will not be discussed in the present paper. It will be sufficient merely to state succinctly the condition of the work in general during the past year.

Missionaries have come and gone, as in former years. Some have been obliged to toil beyond the proper limits of their health and strength. One—a giant amongst us—has fallen. The tall form and kindly face of that veteran missionary, the Rev. G. F. Verbeck, D. D., will never again be seen at this Council.

One of the noticeable features of the work connected with the Council is the wide extent of the field in which the foreign missionaries and Japanese workers are scattered. In greater or less degree, they are spread over almost the length and breadth of the Empire—from Kyushu to the Hokkaido. Though this wide distribution of the working force may have its

9

advantages in the way of varied experience and other wise, still it is a question whether more effective work could not be done by somewhat concentrating our efforts in a field of less extended limits. By drawing more closely together geographically, the Co-operating Missions might conserve much energy that is now expended without corresponding returns Unnecessary duplication of work could be avoided and combinations could be made for the thorough management of a smaller number of better equipped educational institutions at less expense in missionaries and money. Other things being equal, if our large working force were more compact, besides minor advantages, there would in all probability be a deeper impression made upon the general status of society within the field of operations than now, so that relatively a larger number of converts might reason ably be expected. The most necessary thing to be accomplished from now on is to secure a goodly number of self-supporting and aggressive churches which shall form a sustaining constituency for exist ing Christian schools. But as things are now, it wil be impossible for many years to come, apparently, to obtain such adequate Japanese backing. The in stitutionalism of missionary operations in Japan is o too great proportions to warrant the belief that there will soon be a correspondingly large number of con verts able and willing to sustain existing enterprises Were we less scattered, we might reasonably hope to secure a relatively larger constituency for the institutions reduced in number and expense to actua necessities.

Again, a general survey of the work reveals a great variety in activity. There are, of course training-schools, colleges and seminaries of variou grades. Then we have regular church work; that is the preaching of the Word and the administration o the sacraments. But besides these, almost every honorable method conceivable is tried in order to bring people into the Kingdom of God. There are Christian Endeavor Societies, temperance organizations, Sunday Schools and classes for the study of the Bible, primary schools for poor children, English language classes and schools, stereopticon exhibitions, tent meetings, clubs or associations for young men, meetings for women and children, open air preaching, orphanages, a leper asylum, distribution of tracts Bibles and pictures, sewing circles, knitting classes, groups of Scripture Union members, exposition of the Bible by correspondence, industrial enterprises, special work for juvenile criminals, *jinrikisha* men, cotton mill operatives and policemen, reading rooms, a religious press, etc. Opinions probably differ as to the utility of some of these methods of work. Much of course, depends upon the person employing the method. The same way of doing things succeeds differently with different workers. However, it cannot but be gratifying to the supporters of missions to know that inventive genius and adaptability are not wanting in those who do the actual work. As a rule, any method with a reasonable probability of success to recommend it, needs not long to go a begging for enterprising experimenters to give it a fair trial. Occasionally conventional considerations prevent workers from attempting new modes of procedure, but in Japan the tendency is apt to be towards the other extreme.

In the next place, one cannot but notice the persistent hopefulness of the missionaries. With but rare exceptions, the reports have spoken of the work as in an encouraging condition. The personal element and a variety of circumstances, however, combine to render an exact estimate of the real state of things difficult. Two persons of opposite temperaments and varied experience, with different degrees of judicial ability, may be equally sincere ; but it is altogether likely that their conclusions regarding the same facts will diverge to no small extent. It

11

is but natural, therefore, that some missionaries, in view of the fluctuations in the condition of missionary work, are inclined to take a rather despondent view of the situation; while others see matters in a brighter light. We do not all have - the sense of proportion equally developed. Hence, to some the large number of merely nominal Christians enrolled, the seeking for place and power, the small attendance at the regular services of the sanctuary, unholy living on the part of some members of the Church, and similar undeniable facts, must appeal with overwhelming force. Again, to others, such mournful phenomena appear to be quite in accordance with the usual way of things; and they wonder that under the circumstances the case is not far worse. However, as already intimated, the prevailing tone of the reports is one of encouragement. Taking into consideration the above-mentioned variable factors that enter into the formation of judgments, the prevailing hopefulness on the part of our missionaries is striking. Unfriendly critics of missions have more than broadly hinted that missionaries are given to exaggerate their successes, for the sake of effect upon the home constituency. This, at best, is very superficial and gratuitous. There, is no inherent necessity why missionaries should on the average be less sincere than others; and there is generally speaking a profound significance in the fact that missionaries are hopeful. They are working in a cause that has always been winning conquests over great odds. By the mere process of heredity, as well as through conscious faith, they have developed a fixed habit of never completely losing heart. This, no doubt, unconsciously influences them in giving an account of their stewardship. Still, allowing for this, we cannot but conclude that the practically unanimous sentiment of encouragement on the part of our missionary force truly indicates the real state of the work in general.

Missionary work, for purposes of convenience, is divided into two general classes : educational and evangelistic. However, these two departments constantly overlap each other ; and indeed are, or ought to be, but different phases of the same work.

Connected with the Co-operating Missions there are three colleges (or schools) with theological departments : Steele College in Nagasaki (Reformed Church of America), the Meiji Gakuin in Tokyo (Reformed Church of America and Presbyterian Church in the U. S. A.), and the Tohoku Gakuin in Sendai (Reformed Church in the United States). All three institutions suffer from a falling off in theological students. Steel College has an increased attendance in the academic department, but its theological department is temporarily closed because the small number of students remaining declined to return unless a foreign teacher were provided. For the falling off in the attendance of theological students at the Meiji Gakuin, Dr. Imbrie mentions three reasons : The smaller number of additions to the church in recent years, especially among young men ; the increasing opportunities for business life ; and the policy of the missions looking to the employment of a smaller number of workers. The causes mentioned by Dr. Imbrie may operate at the Tohoku Gakuin also ; but it ought to be said in addition that there has been a falling off in the attendance of collegiate students, upon whom the theological department largely depends for its supply.

Mission colleges are at a great disadvantage on account of the great privileges conferred by the Government upon its own schools. Exemption from military conscription and official positions after graduation are prizes which draw to the Government schools multitudes of young men who are at all able by hook or crook to obtain entrance. Mission schools are often used by these young aspirants as stepping stones to the Government colleges. Some of the Japanese connected with mission schools, seeing this state of things, and impressed with the idea that an educational institution is not prosperous unless it has a large number of students, are disposed to agitate in favor of compliance with the conditions required by the Government for securing the coveted privileges. It is to be hoped that the colleges for young men connected with this Council will stand firm for perfect freedom in definite Christian propagandism through the agency of schools, in the hope that public sentiment will demand of the Educational Department equal privileges for all schools of equal grade, irrespective of religious considerations. The recent journalistic discussion concerning the Doshisha case has led at least one of the Japanese newspapers to make this demand ; and we hope to see the day when the justice of it will be substantially recognized.

Japanese facilities for the education of young women is pitiably disproportionate to those provided for young men. A high official—the Vice Minister —of the Educational Department not long ago acknowledged that at present the education of woman is mostly in the hands of the missionaries. There is thus a rich field open as yet to foreign lady missionaries. Public interest in the education of women is bound to increase in time. The Japanese are too keen not to recognize the ruinous consequences of neglecting the women of the country. Meanwhile, however, lady missionaries have a golden opportunity. Japanese girls are apt to be more steady in their attendance, and are in some respects better subjects for continuous religious influence than boys.

There is quite an imposing list of mission colleges (or schools) for girls and young women. A flourishing school is conducted in Yokohama by the Womans

Union Mission. The Cumberland Presbyterian Mission has the Wilmina Girls School in Osaka. In Nagoya there is the Kinjo Jo Gakko under the patronage of the Southern Presbyterian Mission. The Reformed Church of America supports two schools for girls; Sturges Seminary in Nagasaki and Ferris Seminary in Yokohama. The Naniwa Jo Gakko in Osaka, the Hokusei Jo Gakko in Sapporo, the Kōjō Jo Gakuin in Yamaguchi, the Kanazawa Girls School, and the Joshi Gakuin in Tokyo, are fostered by the Northern Presbyterian Mission. The Reformed Church in the United States supports the Miyagi Jo Gakko in Sendai. In all these much emphasis is placed upon Bible study; and were it not for opposition from relatives or guardians, public professions of faith on the part of pupils would be more numerous than now. Many of the best Sunday School teachers are drawn from the ranks of the Christian pupils in these schools.

The outlook for the future of the school of the Womans Union Mission is bright and the teachers are greatly encouraged. At Sturges Seminary examinations have caused an improvement in the attendance at the Bible classes. Ferris Seminary has been re-organized. It is now of a lower grade than formerly, and a special two years' Bible course has been provided. The attendance has been the smallest in seventeen years, but the spirit of both teachers and pupils is earnest and devout. At the Naniwa Jo Gakko a large temperance society has been organized. The Hokusei Jo Gakko has had a good attendance; and nearly all of the older girls are Christians. At Yamaguchi a regiment of soldiers was recently stationed. Since then the Kōjō Gakuin has been attended by daughters of military officers; but they are transients, and it is almost impossible to produce any religious impression upon them during their short stay. A revival of interest in the education of women and a new friendliness toward Christianity are supposed to be indicated by the large

15

influx of new students at the Joshi Gakuin. These new pupils however are apt to leave after a few weeks' experience of the hard work required. The Wilmina Girls School in Osaka and the Miyagi Jo Gakko in Sendai have had a quiet year of steady work undisturbed by any incidents of special importance.

In addition to these boarding schools for young men and women, there is a number of day schools which do an important work. To this class belong the Kyodokwan in Okazaki; the Taisei Upper Primary School in Yokohama; the Seishu Jo Gakko in Otaru; two schools for poor children, the one in Kagoshima and the other in Yokohama; the Keimo Primary Schools, Nos. I. and II. and that at Shinagawa, in Tokyo; two day schools connected with the Naniwa Jo Gakko in Osaka; and the school for children at Kanazawa.

Of Bible training-schools there are four. Mrs. L. H. Pierson speaks of the school at No. 212, Bluff, Yokohama, as having been greatly blessed during the past year in spite of some discouraging experiences that were entirely new. The school at Tsu, Ise, under the oversight of Mrs. A. M. Drennan, has had a prosperous year. Graduates are required to work for one year in the immediate vicinity of the school. Afterwards they are allowed to go elsewhere. Miss Couch conducts a small Bible training-class for women in Nagasaki. In Tokyo Mrs. MacNair and Miss West have a school, the great usefulness of which has been somewhat circumscribed by lack of sufficient funds.

EVANGELISTIC WORK.

The field of operations being so extensive, the condition of the work, naturally enough, is not uniform throughout. The Hokkaido is perhaps the readiest to receive the Gospel. There is very little,

16

if any, opposition there ; and, the country being new, the people are more hospitably inclined to a new religion. The power of old associations is broken, and the residents are freer to act on their own responsibility than in places where fixed customs and conventionalities still hold sway. Here the outlook is very bright indeed. Tohoku (the north-east) is regarded by the Japanese themselves as a section rather indifferent to religious matters. Temples are comparatively few. Christianity here is not making very rapid progress, but opposition is not very pronounced. In fact, where the prevailing lethargy has yielded somewhat, it is not difficult to secure large and attentive audiences. Other sections of the empire occupied by our missionaries are gradually becoming better acquainted with Christianity, and prejudice is slowly but surely giving way. Not a few cases of illegal interference with Christian work on the part of public school teachers have been reported. However, a persistent exposure of such misdoings is very likely to put a stop to them. Buddhist priests sometimes bestir themselves sufficiently to canvass a town to exact pledges from the people that they will not attend Christian meetings ; but as often perhaps some of these functionaries are to be found themselves listening to Christian sermons.

During the year several prominent professors in the Imperial University at Tokyo have undertaken to give religious impetus to Japanese life by rehabilitating old Shintoistic ideas under the name of Japanese Principles. This has led to considerable writing in newspapers and magazines ; but, unless appearances are deceiving, Nipponism has had no appreciable effect upon our work.

The near approach of Mixed Residence furnishes workers with a good text for Christian preaching. There is a feeling that preparation must be made for meeting the new conditions. As foreigners are expected by many of the Japanese to flock into the interior of the country, beginning with July of next year, the people are urged to acquaint themselves with the religion of the foreigners. Evangelists also are supposed to be under especial obligations to preach the Gospel as widely as possible, in anticipation of certain evil as well as good effects that are expected to follow the influx of foreigners. On the other hand, Buddhist priests use the sure prospect of Mixed Residence as a reason why the people should beware of Christianity and foreign Christians.

Last November the Church of Christ in Japan celebrated the twenty-fifth anniversary of its organization. As a fitting way of commemorating this noteworthy event in the history of the Church, the Japanese Christians held special evangelistic services in different parts of the country.

Among the various methods of evangelistic work carried on by different missionaries, that pursued by the Rev. J. B. Hail is worthy of special consideration. Mr. Hail says : " It seems to me that the work of keeping the church in line is that of the pastor of the church and his session. I myself do no pastoral work unless I am invited to do it. My work is with outsiders. It is going from house to house and presenting the Gospel to the head of the house. I visit every house, announce my name and business. I spend no time in conversation aside from the matter in hand. When I have presented the essential truths, which occupies from fifteen minutes to two or three hours as the case may be, I usually leave a tract and an invitation to our church services. I visit from one to fifteen houses per day. As a rule I am well received, and people listen to the Gospel."

Another method is that recently pursued by the Rev. Geo. W. Fulton. This method is thus described by the Rev. W. Y. Jones. " Mr. Fulton's desire was to reach the class of persons who are interested in Christianity but shrink from the publicity that comes from personal contact with either the Japanese evangelist or the foreign missionary. His plan is briefly this. Each week a passage of Scripture, with a short commentary thereon, is mimeographed in Japanese. Once a month, for the space of three or four days, an advertisement is inserted in the Fukui daily papers, offering to send this mimeographed exposition to any who are willing to receive it. The number of those studying by this method has gradually increased ; the whole number now being about ninety. Of these, the greater number are in Fukui City and the immediate vicinity ; but some are scattered along the western coast of Japan from Kanazawa to Tsuruga, and others are in Yamaguchi Ken, Kyoto and Yokohama. Many letters are received asking questions concerning Christianity suggested by the correspondence. To these reply is made, and appropriate tracts forwarded to meet their needs. Already deep impressions have been made, and it seems evident that such a method has its place."

After all has been said the fact remains that Christianity is surely winning its way into the hearts of the people. The words of the Rev. A. Oltmans with reference to his own field seem of such general application that, as a fitting conclusion to this report, they are quoted at length.

" There is a growing interest in Christianity *at large ;* more toleration for it, and a deepening conviction among thinking Japanese that Christianity is superior to any other religious system they know of in Japan. The number of those who have come in contact with and have been to some extent influenced by Christianity is greatly on the increase. We find them in places where one would least expect them. These are approachable if tact and courage are properly combined. The example of some of our Christians is telling in the way of testimony upon even such as have as yet no earnest desire to become Christians themselves. Our Christians have many things to contend with in the way of family, social and business relations that endanger their fervor of faith and earnestness of Christian practice. The fear of man is present to a large degree. This is true still more with those who are favorably inclined towards Christianity. Apparently it is keeping them from making an open confession of what they believe to be the truth."

II.

MEETING OF THE SYNOD

BY THE

Rev. T. T. ALEXANDER, D.D.

The twelfth stated meeting of the Synod was held—
July 14th to 19th—in Van Schaick Hall, Yokohama.
The sessions were opened with a sermon by the retir-
ing Moderator, the Rev. H. Yamamoto, pastor of the
Shiloh Church, from the text, Wherefore, my beloved
brethren, be ye stedfast, unmoveable, always abound-
ing in the work of the Lord. 1. Cor. 15 : 58.

The sermon was a plea for an earnest faith based
upon the truths of Christianity. "Many are prone to
be content if only numbers are added to the Church
from year to year : but this is not the success that
we should seek to attain. What we need to aim at is
the establishment of the fundamental truths of the
Gospel in the hearts of the people. Again, there are
those who are content to rest in a sort of idealistic
faith. Christianity, they say, is a spiritual religion.
We need not concern ourselves about the *form* either
in doctrine or in church organization. One form is
as good as another, and all forms are imperfect and
inadequate. If only men will keep fast hold of
Christ, sit at his feet, look to him, all will be well.
There is in this a large element of truth. but at the
same time the position is a dangerous one. Christianity is not subjective only, it is objective also. It

Sermon.

21

rests upon certain well defined and firmly established truths. It is therefore vitally important that each Church should formulate these truths and hold fast to them. The Church of Christ in Japan has a short, simple, and evangelical creed; upon this creed its ministers stand; upon the truths embodied in it they need to lay the greatest emphasis; they should see to it that they are taught, and as far as possible accepted, in the churches over which they have charge; for these truths are essential to an intelligent and Scriptural faith." At the close of the sermon, the Synod proceeded to the election of officers. The Rev. K. Ibuka was chosen Moderator, and the Rev. H. Yamamoto, Clerk.

Statistics.

The Committee on the State of Religion presented its report. According to it, the whole number of the churches connected with the Synod is 71; of preaching places 102; of ordained ministers 88; the whole number of believers 11,131; the number baptized during the year 683; and the total amount of contributions for all purposes *yen* 23,354.41.

Co-operation.

Another report of great interest was that of the Committee on Cooperation. This committee was appointed by the Synod at its previous meeting to confer with the Missions Cooperating with the Church of Christ in Japan with a view to securing cooperation of a closer and more formal character than that existing at present. The committee reported that a conference had been held with representatives of the several missions,* but without at-

---

* For the sake of reference the action of the Council in 1897 regarding cooperation is herewith inserted.

" Whereas the Synod at its late session in Tokyo adopted a minute in regard to the matter of co-operation between the presbyteries and the missions, stating what, in the opinion of the Synod, constitutes true co-operation, and appointed a committee of seven to confer with a similar committee from the Co-operating Missions on the subject, be it

Resolved that in view of individual and widely differing responsibilities, co-operation is, in the opinion of the Council, best carried out where the Japanese Church organization, in its sessions, presbyteries and Synod,

taining the result desired. The missions, though not averse to cooperation in a general and some what vague sense of the word, were nevertheless unwilling to cooperate upon the plan suggested by the Synod. The committee regarded this as unfortunate, and had used every means in its power to reach a satisfactory conclusion in the matter, but in vain. It was, therefore, with regret that it was constrained to report that the Cooperating Missions are unwilling to cooperate, in any formal or official sense of the term. At the same time, the committee did not forget the great work done by the missions in the past, and recognized the work still being carried on by them. It also recognized the value of cooperation of this informal and moral kind. In conclusion, there seemed at present no course open to the Synod but for it and the missions to go on very much as at present, each party working on its own lines. The committee suggested however that hereafter, as a matter of information, the statistical tables indicate in some way what work is done by the Synod and what by the missions.

A prolonged discussion followed the presentation of this report. A large majority of the Synod was in favour of simply accepting it and allowing the matter to rest. The minority, however, strenuously insisted that the question was one of the greatest importance, and that a committee should be appointed to negotiate further with the missions, and

---

directs all ecclesiastical matters, availing itself of the counsels and assistance of the missions or missionaries as occasion arises ; while the missions direct their own educational, evangelistic and other missionary operations, availing themselves, likewise, of whatever counsel and assistance they may be able to obtain from their brethren in the Japanese Church ; and that under these circumstances, it does not seem best to enter into co-operation as defined by the Synod ; but to recommend that a committee be appointed of one from each mission to confer with the committee of the Synod in a spirit of fraternal good will, for the purpose of communicating the opinion of the Council and endeavoring to promote a better understanding on the subject of co-operation."

if possible secure cooperation of a more definite kind and more in accordance with the views of the Synod. Finally it was decided to refer the whole matter to a committee with instructions to consider the subject carefully and recommend what action should be taken. At a later session, the committee thus appointed presented in the following resolutions, which were adopted by a large majority :—

Resolved 1. That the Synod express its thanks to the Committee on Cooperation and direct that its report be printed in the Minutes.

2. That, inasmuch as it appears that the Synod and the Council of Missions differ in opinion regarding the wisest method of cooperation, further consideration of the subject be postponed for the present.

3. That although unhappily it has not been possible to reach an agreement regarding the method of cooperation, the Church of Christ in Japan recognizes its great obligation to the missions, and holds that the relations between it and them should be those of cordial friendship and mutual helpfulness.

While these resolutions were adopted by a vote that was nearly unanimous, a small minority was still urgent for some further action. On two points in particular they pressed for a decision. In their view the position that the co-operation between the Synod and the missions is not formal or official necessarily affects the position of churches and preaching places receiving financial aid from the missions, and also raises the question of the propriety of missionaries sitting as advisory members of the presbyteries and the Synod. The first of these points the Synod decided was sufficiently met by the action already taken that hereafter the statistical tables shall indicate which of the churches and preaching places receive aid from missions or other outside sources. To the second point the Synod answered that any action regarding the position of advisory members would involve an amendment of the Canons which could be effected only in the constitutional way. A resolution however was adopted directing the presbyteries to see that the terms of the Canon (Can. 23 : § 6) are strictly complied with.

With this the long discussion came to an end. The whole subject is a delicate and complicated one growing out of the transitional stage through which the Church as a whole is now passing. As soon as it is able to assume the entire responsibility, financial and otherwise, the present difficulties will disappear. Meanwhile the situation calls for prudence and forbearance on the part of both the Church and the missions.

The report of the Committee on Presbyterial Records brought up two questions of interest. It appeared that in the Naniwa Presbytery a company of *Care of companies of believers.* believers had been put under the care of a committee composed of private church members. This action the Synod declared to be irregular; such care including "that ordinarily exercised by a session" (Can. 1.). The second question grew out of an action of the Miyagi Presbytery. For certain reasons that presbytery had adopted a resolution exscinding a number of preaching places connected with it. Happily the question was no longer a practical one, *Excision of companies of believers.* the connection between the presbytery and the companies of believers having been re-established. The committee however while recognizing the fact that the circumstances might seem in a measure to justify the action of the presbytery, expressed the judgment that the action was unwarranted. In this opinion the Synod concurred.

A case of appeal worthy of notice came before the Synod. An elder in the Ushigome Church had become convinced that immersion is the only proper *Mode of baptism.* form of baptism. He therefore had himself immersed and then proceeded to teach in the Sunday School that baptism by sprinkling is not baptism at all.

The session took the matter up and decided to remove him from his office as elder. From this decision he appealed to the presbytery. The presbytery sustained the action of the session ; and from that decision he appealed to the Synod. The report of the Judicial Committee on the case, which was adopted by the Synod, was as follows :—

" The mode of baptism differs in different Churches. In the Oriental Churches the common mode is immersion ; in the Roman Catholic Church, the Church of England, the Lutheran Church, and in the Presbyterian and Reformed Churches, the common mode is sprinkling. The Church of Christ in Japan, as most of the Churches of Christ throughout the world, holds that the mode is not essential ; both immersion and sprinkling are valid. To insist upon a different view is to oppose the great principle of Christian liberty and to make Christianity a religion of forms, which is contrary to the spirit of the New Testament. The Church of Christ in Japan has great respect for the rights of conscience. It is for this very reason that it insists that the mode of baptism shall not be made an essential. In all matters, excepting those immediately connected with the fundamental truths of Christianity, it will ever exercise the utmost forbearance towards any of its members who hold their views in such a way as not to disturb the peace of the Church. But to hold and teach that persons should be re-baptized has a manifest tendency to divide the Church into parties and to destroy the spirit of love. An officer, or private member, who deems it his duty to propagate such views should apply for dismission to some other Church with whose principles he is in harmony.

The Synod therefore confirms the decision of the presbytery."

Dr. Verbeck. Appropriate resolutions in reference to the death of Dr. Verbeck were adopted, to be recorded in the Minutes and sent to the bereaved family. The

26

application of the First and Second Presbyteries of Tokyo to be united was approved. A committee was appointed to prepare a pastoral letter to be sent to all ministers, evangelists, and sessions, urging upon them the importance of looking carefully after church members who change their residence, and of seeing that they carry with them letters to other churches connected with the Church of Christ in Japan. A committee of three was also appointed to consider the method of Church Sustentation now in operation in the Free Church of Scotland, and to report on the wisdom of adopting some such plan for the Church of Christ in Japan. This touches a matter of prime importance—the care and upbuilding of the weaker churches. The committee is to report at the next stated meeting of the Synod.

The great importance of the evangelistic work of the Church gives to the report of the Board of Home Missions a place second to nothing in the business of the Synod.

The Board consists of twenty members, one half of whom are elected at each stated meeting of the Synod. Care is always taken to secure a thoroughly representative body of men, so that every presbytery is represented in the Board. The management of financial matters and of the work in general is, however, entrusted to an Executive Committee residing in Tokyo and Yokohama. Hitherto the fiscal year has extended from July 1st to June 30th ; but hereafter it will correspond to the calendar year.

For the year just ended the Board was authorized to raise the sum of *yen* 3,600. The amount actually raised was 2,891.15. There was, however, at the beginning of the year a balance in hand of 4.45. There was also in hand 65.36 ; a balance from a fund raised for the purpose of sending a committee to Formosa. This balance the Synod authorized the Board to expend upon its regular work.

Adding these balances to the amount raised during the year, the entire sum at the disposal of the Board was 2,960.96. The sum expended was 2,892.69; leaving a balance at the end of the year of 68.27.

Work.
During the past year work has been carried on at Ueda and Minami-Kita Saku Gun, in the Province of Shinshu; at Mito, Ota-mura, and Shimotsuma in Ibaraki Ken; and at Taihoku and Tainan, in Formosa. From these centres it branches out in various directions and is gradually assuming larger proportions.

The work at Tainan, which was begun a little more than a year ago, has gone on under difficulties. It has had from the start the sympathy and generous assistance of the missionaries of the English Presbyterian Church, who are working there. But unfortunately the Rev. Mr. Hirayama, who was sent there by the Board, was compelled to return to this part of the empire on account of the serious illness of his wife. He returned last spring and the Rev. R. Hosokawa, until recently pastor of the Kaigan Church in Yokohama, has been sent to take his place. Those who know Mr. Hosokawa will feel a deep interest in his work, sympathize with him in his separation from home and friends, and follow him with their prayers. He is an earnest and consecrated man, well fitted for the work he has undertaken.

The present report, as compared with that of last year, shows a falling off in the number of baptisms; the whole number for the year being only thirty-two. Of these, seven were in Taihoku and the vicinity; twenty-two in Ueda; and three in Ibaraki Ken. In Taihoku there are many inquirers, as also in Minami-Kita Saku Gun; and it is expected that a considerable number will be baptized in all these places before long.

Sources of receipts.
As already stated, the sum received by the Board during the year was *yen* 2891.15. The sources from

28

which this amount was obtained appear in the following table :—

Churches and places under care of the Board	... ...	363.80
Other churches and preaching places	... ...	945.94
Individuals (Japanese) ...	... ...	802.75
Missionaries in Formosa	... ...	250.00
„ in Japan proper...	... ...	159.00
Woman's Societies (Japanese)	... ...	93.09
Methodist Protestant Church for work in Formosa	...	25.72
Japanese church in San Francisco...	... ...	25.51
Raised in connection with special meetings in celebration of the 25th anniversary of the Church	... ...	225.34
Total...		2,891 15

The fear has sometimes been expressed that the work of the Board is carried on largely by contributions from churches and preaching places receiving financial aid from the missions, which might be regarded as a case of robbing Peter to pay Paul. A glance at the statistics shows that such fears are not well founded. The following list contains twenty-one churches and four preaching places. Of these one church alone—that at Kyoto—is dependent upon the missions for financial support ; and that church pays half of its pastor's salary and all incidental expenses. All the other churches and preaching places in the list are financially independent of the missions. In some cases the figures include contributions by members of the churches made directly to the Board.

Churches :									yen
Taihoku ...	...	...	...	...	...	...	...	...	130.00
Ueda...	...	...	...	...	...	...	...	...	85.10
Kaigan	...	...	...	...	...	...	...	...	80.00
Kochi	...	...	...	...	...	...	...	...	72.00
Ichi Bancho	...	...	...	...	...	...	...	...	57.09
Shiloh	...	...	...	...	...	...	...	...	46.85
Nagoya ...	...	...	...	...	...	...	...	...	37.78
Daimachi	...	...	...	...	...	...	...	...	35.30
Yamaguchi	...	...	...	...	...	...	...	...	33.75
Shinsakai	...	...	...	...	...	...	...	...	33.01
Hakodate	...	...	...	...	...	...	...	...	27.82
Sapporo ...	...	...	...	...	...	...	...	...	27.00
Kyoto	...	...	...	...	...	...	...	...	25.89

									yen
Nagasaki ...	...	...	...	...	...	...	.-	...	23.21
Kojimachi	...	...	...	...	...	...	...	...	16.00
Osaka South	...	...	...	..	...	...	...	...	12.77
Chiba	...	...	...	...	...	...	...	...	12.00
Shitaya ...	...	...	...	...	...	...	...	...	11.64
Hongo	...	...	...	...	...	...	...	...	11.50
Osaka North	...	...	...	...	...	...	..•	...	10.00
Seigen	...	...	...	...	...	...	...	...	10.00

Preaching places :

Minami Saku Gun ...	...	...	...	...	...	...	50.00
Two places in Ibaraki Ken	...	...	...	...	...	71.07
Ichigaya ...	...	...	...	...	...	...	12.05
Aki ...	...	...	...	...	...	...	10.20

In short, a careful examination of the figures shows that only a comparatively small proportion of the income of the Board was from churches or preaching places directly connected with the missions. Probably from ten to fifteen per cent.

Another fear sometimes expressed is that the *Self-support.* policy of the Board tends to hinder rather that to promote self-support. To bring a congregation of believers to *real* self-support—to the point where it pays a pastor a proper salary ; erects and maintains a suitable building, and carries on an active work, is no easy task. How difficult a task those alone know who have succeeded in the endeavor. In the opinion of the Board the *timely* and *judicious* use of money is a great aid to the securing of the end in view. It believes that such aid encourages the believers and helps them to the point where they are able and willing to take care of themselves and to assist others. From the beginning it has been the *aim* of the Board to push self-support as rapidly as possible ; and its experience has been such as to encourage it. The Church at Ueda, which has been for some two years under the care of the Board, has become self-supporting. It has received no aid since the end of March, pays its pastor twenty-five *yen* a month, and defrays all other expenses. The work in Minami and Kita Saku Gun also, has become self-supporting ; paying the salary of the minister and all other expenses. These churches both lie in a region in which the missionaries of the Reformed (Dutch) Church have long labored, and in taking charge of them the Board entered into their labors. The church at Taihoku in Formosa, which now pays one half the pastor's salary, will it is hoped become self-supporting at no very distant day. The believers there, however, are at present making strenuous efforts to build a chapel ; and this may delay progress in the direction of self-support. The Board has recently taken under its care the church at Kobe. The church with the aid of missionaries residing in the place has agreed to assume a large share of the expenses at the start. It is the hope of the Board that such kindly aid may not long be needed.

The estimate for the work of the year, as approved by the Synod, is *yen* 3,700. From one point of view that is a small thing. But let us not despise the day of small things. It is to such institutions as this Board that in the end will be given in a great degree the evangelization of the empire.

Estimate for next year.

III.

PROCEEDINGS

CF THE

TWENTY-FIRST ANNUAL MEETING
OF THE COUNCIL.

---

1. DEVOTIONAL EXERCISES.

The Council of Missions Cooperating with the Church of Christ in Japan assembled in Karuizawa, at 9 A. M., July 21st, 1898. The sessions were opened with a sermon by the President, the Rev. T. M. Mac Nair, from the text, Hold fast the form of sound words, which thou hast heard of me, in faith and love which is in Christ Jesus. The meetings for business every morning were preceded by a prayer service led by members of the Council or visiting friends. Early morning meetings also were held. The evenings were occupied by Bible readings given by Dr. Geo. C. Needham ; and from time to time Mrs. Needham addressed the ladies.

2. MEMORIAL SERVICE.

On Sunday afternoon a special service was held in memory of Dr. Verbeck, who entered into rest since the last meeting of the Council greatly beloved and deeply lamented. At this service, Mr. Mac Nair presided ; the Scriptures were read by Mr. E. Rothesay Miller; prayer was offered by Dr. Scott of the Canadian Methodist Mission and Mr. Dearing of the American Baptist Mission; and addresses* were delivered by Dr. Thompson and Mr. Oltmans, and by Dr. Learned of the American Board and Dr. Ashmore of the American Baptist Mission. The service was marked for its simple dignity and tender Christian feeling.

3. COMMUNICATIONS AND CORRESPONDENCE.

A resolution adopted by the Conference of the Church Missionary Society, expressive of the deep loss sustained by the Churches of Christ in Japan in the death of Bishop Bickersteth, Archdeacon Maundrell and Dr. Verbeck, was read before the Council. The communication with its accompanying letter was entered upon the Minutes, and the Secretary was directed to reply in fitting terms of thanks and sympathy. `Church Miss. Society and Dr. Verbeck.`

A letter was read from Dr. Moore of the German Reformed Mission, who was lying seriously ill in Karuizawa, conveying the warm Christian greetings of the writer, assuring the Council of his deep sympathy and constant prayer, and requesting a like return in his own behalf. The Council directed the letter to be inserted in the Minutes; and a reply was sent to Dr. Moore expressing the deep feeling of the Council on hearing his letter read, and pledging itself to remember him in prayer from day to day. `Dr. Moore.`

The Rev. H. K. Miller presented the following reply from the missionaries in Formosa in response to the greetings of the Council.† `Missionaries in Formosa.`

---

* For an outline of the addresses delivered, See IV.
† The letter of the Council to the missionaries in Formosa is inserted from the Proceedings of last year.

33

Karuizawa, Japan, July 17th, 1897.

Dear Brethren :

In view of the fact that, by the incorporation of Formosa into the Empire of Japan, two missions have been added to the number of those whose ecclesiastical organization is Presbyterial in principle, we, the Council of the Missions Co-operating with the Church of Christ in Japan, hereby extend to the Missions of the Canadian and English Presbyterian Churches in Formosa our most cordial Christian greetings. The best wishes of the Council, now in annual session at Karuizawa, go out to the missionaries in Formosa in the hope that their labors for the extension of Christ's kingdom may continue to be crowned with abundant success.

It would be highly gratifying to the Council if the two missions just mentioned would become regular members of the Council and send representatives to its annual meetings. If the way is not yet open for this, any suggestions contemplating the establishing and continuance of cordial relations between the Presbyterian missionaries in Formosa and the Council will be heartly welcomed.

The grace of our Lord Jesus Christ be with you all. Amen.

English Presbyterian Mission,
Tainanfu, Formosa,
2nd May, 1898.

Dear Brethren :

I duly received your fraternal letter of greeting of date July 17, 1897. On my return from Japan last year I sought an opportunity of laying it before my colleagues ; but as, owing to illness and other causes, we were at that time very much scattered it was several months before I succeeded in doing so. I was imstructed to reply, returning you thanks for your kind wishes, and expressing, in return our best wishes that all prosperity may be granted to you in the

34

carrying on of your work. You will be glad to know that, in spite of the disturbed condition of the country and the anxious state of men's minds, the year that has closed has in several ways been the most successful we have had for long. The number of adult admissions was 158, the largest I remember in twenty-three years of missionary life. Total communicants 1899. Money contributions half as much again as in previous years ; going up from about $ 2,400 to $ 3,700. About two years ago we established our Presbytery here, and this year in April ordained our first two native ministers. As in our mission, both in Formosa and on the mainland of China, we make it a rule that all moneys for the native ministers, whether for salary or expenses, must be raised by the native Christians without any help from abroad, we have been rather slower than some missions in the work of ordination. It may prove to be wise delay in the long run.

As regards entering into closer relations with your Council we do not see our way to propose anything in the meantime. The distance and expense prevent the possibility of sending a representative to attend meetings of your Council. Visits paid on the score of health are generally paid later in the year than the time of your meeting. Besides which our work is still so purely Chinese and so little affected even externally by the political changes that have taken place, that we do not as yet feel much sense of unity with the Japanese Church and Missions, though this feeling will doubtless grow with time, and result in more active co-operation.

With greetings to the members of your Council,
I remain, Yours very truly,

THOMAS BARCLAY.

The following letter was received in reply to the greetings of the Council conveyed through a committee :— Wom. Miss. Soc. of the Can. Meth. Church.

Karuizawa, July 21st, 1898.

The members of the Council of the Womans Missionary Society of the Canadian Methodist Church in Japan, now in session in Karuizawa, extend to the Cooperating Missions their most cordial greetings. Now the Lord of peace himself give you peace always by all means. The Lord be with you all. 2 Thess. 3 : 16.

I. S. BLACKMORE.
C. E. HART.

Temperance Sunday.

A communication from Miss Clara Parrish was presented, calling attention to the fact that the last Sunday in November had been adopted by a number of the missions in Japan as Temperance Sunday. The Council recommended that the day be observed.

Unfermented wine at the Communion.

A letter from Miss E. A. Preston was received inquiring regarding the use of unfermented wine at the Communion in the churches connected with the Church of Christ in Japan. The Council directed that a reply be sent to Miss Preston, suggesting the advisability of communicating directly with the Rev. H. Yamamoto, Clerk of the Synod.

4. REPORTS OF SPECIAL COMMITTEES APPOINTED BY THE LAST COUNCIL.

General report of the work of the year.

The General Report of the work of the year was read by the Rev. H. K. Miller. A resolution of thanks to Mr. Miller was adopted; and the Publications Committee was authorized to print and distribute one thousand copies of the report in the usual manner.

Cooperation.

The committee, appointed by the several missions* to confer with the Committee on Cooperation appointed by the Synod, gave a verbal account of the conference, and also of the discussion of the matter at the

* See footnote on page 22.

recent meeting of the Synod. † The committee also presented the action of the Synod, which was as follows :—

RESOLVED 1. That the Synod express its thanks to the Committee on Cooperation, and direct that its report be printed in the Minutes.

2. That inasmuch as it appears that the Synod and the Council of the Missions differ in opinion regarding the wisest method of cooperation, further consideration of the subject be postponed for the present.

3. That although unhappily it has not been possible to reach an agreement regarding the method of cooperation, the Church of Christ in Japan recognizes its great obligations to the missions, and holds that the relations between it and them should be those of cordial friendship and mutual helpfulness.

4. That the Clerk of the Synod be directed to transmit a copy of these resolutions to the Secretaries of the several missions.

The report of the committee having been heard, a special committee was appointed to prepare resolutions with reference to the matter. The special committee presented the following resolutions which were adopted :—

RESOLVED 1. That the Council expresses regret that a difference of opinion exists between the missions and the Synod as to the method of cooperation, but agrees with the Synod that further discussion of the question for the present is unadvisable.

2. That the Council reciprocates the feelings expressed in the third resolution of the Synod, and re-affirms the position that has always been occupied by the missions composing it, which is to cultivate friendship and to assist one another.

---

† See account of the meeting of the Synod, pages 22-24.

3. That the Secretary of the Council be instructed to send an English copy and a Japanese translation of these resolutions to the Clerk of the Synod.

Subsequently the following resolutions bearing on the subject were adopted by the Council:—

RESOLVED 1. That we pledge ourselves to heartfelt, faithful and continual prayer for the whole work committed to the Church of Christ in Japan and the Co-operating Missions.

2. That this resolution be sent to the Synod and to the *Fukuin Shimpo*.

5. REPORTS OF STANDING COMMITTEES AND THE TREASURER.

Publications. The Publications Committee presented its report, which was adopted. During the past year the Annual Report of the Council for 1897 was printed and distributed; the Sunday School Lessons prepared by the Rev. E. Rothesay Miller, and the Yorokobi no Otozure by Mrs. Miller, have appeared regularly. The following books have been published:—

An Exposition of the Book of Genesis, by the Rev. T. M. Mac Nair.

A Commentary on Ephesians, by the Rev. R. B. Grinnan, D. D.

Fifine (a translation), by Mrs. T. M. MacNair.

Catechumens Guide, by the Rev. G. G. Hudson.

The Catechumens Guide is published privately: the other works are issued by the Meth. Pub. House.

Statistics. The Committee on Statistics presented a report elucidated by the accompanying table (page 40) which was prepared from the Annual Table of Statistics. The report was adopted with the following recommendations:—

RESOLVED 1. That the committee thoroughly revise and make more definite both the church and mission statistical tables; keeping in view also the blanks sent out from America.

2. That great care be taken in filling out mission blanks, so as to secure entire accuracy.

3. That a Committee of Ten be appointed to collect statistics; the committee to represent the ten following places, and the whole field to be apportioned accordingly, viz.—Sapporo, Sendai, Tokyo (2), Kanazawa, Nagoya, Osaka, Hiroshima, Kochi, Nagasaki.

4. That the two members representing Tokyo be constituted a central sub-committee to receive, revise, tabulate and publish the blanks.

5. That overtures be made by this sub-committee, looking towards co-operation with the Synod's Committee on Statistics, and also with Mr. Loomis.

In accordance with this recommendation the following Committee of Ten was appointed: For Sapporo, G. P. Pierson; Sendai, H. K. Miller; Tokyo, Henry M. Landis and M. N. Wyckoff; Kanazawa, H. Brokaw; Nagoya, C. K. Cummings; Osaka, J. B. Porter; Hiroshima, A. V. Bryan; Kochi, J. W. Moore; Nagasaki, A. Pieters.

AVERAGE PER COMMUNICANT (yen.)

PRESBYTERY	Total of communicants.	Added on confession.	Sunday School pupils	Total Japanese contributions.	Total Japanese contributions.	Contributions to Bd. Home Missions.	Recd. from foreign sources.	Recd from Bd. and Coms. of Home Miss.	Recd. from all Souces.
Tokyo (1)	3179	220	1479	5833.	1.83	.19	1.35	.06	1.41
Tokyo (2).	1672	94	820	2896	1.74	.10	.36	.15	.51
Miyagi	1296	155	1965	3523.	2.72	.24	4.85	.92	5.77
Naniwa	2431	268	2376	5823.	2.40	.19	4.24	.05	4.29
Sanyo	430	34	321	867.	2.02	.22	7.12	.13	7.25
Chinzei	561	41	441	1425.	2.54	.28	12.09	.15	12.24
Total or General Averages	9631	812	7402	20530.	2.14	.18	3.25	.19	3.44

Meeting places.	Communicants and baptized children.	Adults baptized	S. S. Teachers.	Pastors and evangelists.	Churches.	Preaching places.	Self-supporting churches.	Bible women.	Japanese teachers.	Sunday Schools.
652	10906	730	604	202	69	1.69	22	191	196	274

Stations.	Out-stations.	Day schools.	Pupils in same.	Boys high schools.	Pupils in same.	Girls high schools.	Pupils in same.	Theo. schools.	Theo. students.	Bible women schools.	Bible women students
35	230	15	1155	4	288	11	619	3	42	4	159

The Committee on Self-support appointed by the
Council in 1897* presented its report which was
adopted as follows :—

The following questions were sent to all the sta-
tions of the Cooperating Missions. The answers are
appended in substance.

QUESTION. Has your mission adopted the recommendations of the Council with or without modifi-
tions?

ANSWERS. *East Japan Pres. Mission :*—The mission has not yet, as a mission, considered the recommendations of the Council. *West Japan Pres. Mission :*—The report of the Council was adopted with
the following changes : No. 2 was erased and No. 3 was
modified. *Southern Pres. Mission :*—Adopted with
a slight modification in No. 3. *Cumberland Pres.
Mission :*—Adopted at a mission meeting held in
March 1898. *North Japan Reformed Mission :*—No
formal adoption of the recommendations, but it was

---

* For the sake of reference the action of the Council in 1897 regarding
self-support is herewith inserted

Resolved (1). That all missions co-operating in this Council make it
a rule not to aid financially any church organized hereafter ; and that, in
concurrence with the recent action of Synod on this subject, we earnestly
labor and pray for the entire self-support of all organized churches now
receiving financial aid from the missions, within the next two years.

(2). That in aiding companies of believers, both such as are connected
with organized churches and such as are not, the missions adopt a uniform rule of not paying rent or incidental expenses.

(3). That in all new work, and as far as practicable in already existing
work, the missions be urged to make a trial of Dr. Nevius' method in the
general work of evangelization : Employing fewer workers, paying no
rent or incidental expenses : and by grouping Christians into circuits, to
make the work entirely self-supporting from the very start.

(4). That in all cases churches and preaching places receiving mission
aid be required to fill out a monthly blank showing membership, attendance, amount and sources of all money received, and the manner in which
the same has been expended ; and that this blank be a uniform one for all
the Co-operating Missions.

(5). Finally that the Council appoint a standing Committee of three
members on Self-support, to which any matter relating to the subject may
be referred, and which shall report to the next meeting of the Council.

left to the missionaries in charge to carry them out. *South Japan Reformed Mission:*—Adopted a set of resolutions endorsing the spirit of the recommendations of the Council. *German Reformed Mission:* —Not formally adopted, because at the meeting of Council four representatives of the mission were present and voted for the recommendations. Hence the necessity of a formal adoption did not occur to the mission. *Mission of the United Pres. Church of Scotland:*—No Report. *Womans Union Missionary Society:*—The recommendations are not applicable to our work.

QUESTION. To what extent have the principles been put into operation?

ANSWERS. *East Japan Pres. Mission:*—Apart from the recommendations of the Council, the heavy cut on the estimates of the mission had reduced the number of evangelists at least one-third; and as a result some grouping of churches and companies of believers has taken place. *West Japan Pres. Mission:*—The plan has been put into operation in Kanazawa thoroughly, two men out of five having been dismissed; in the Yamaguchi field seven out of seventeen evangelists have been dismissed, and the rent of preaching places has been reduced from 26 *yen* to 19 *yen* per month; in the Hiroshima field a strong spirit of self-support has been developed. *Southern Pres. Mission:*—The plan, as modified in No. 3, has been put into full operation excepting in the case of two preaching places. *Cumberland Pres. Mission:*—No modification resulting thus far. *North Japan Reformed Mission:*—No forced observance required; practically not in operation. *South Japan Reformed Mission:*—Successfully put into operation in a large part of the field, in accordance with the resolutions adopted by the mission. *German Reformed Mission:* —Put into operation as circumstances permitted without any radical changes.

QUESTION. What apparent results for better or worse have followed, in the matter of self-support, and as to success in evangelization?

ANSWERS. General reply of all the missions :—(1.) The time is too short for any definite conclusions, but most of the fields report favorable progress. (2.) Though the number of workers has been reduced in most of the fields, the same amount of work seems to have been carried on, and the outlook is promising.

QUESTION. Have you any suggestions to make on the general subject?

ANSWERS. The following points are emphasized : —Greater consecration on the part of the Japanese Christians; the need of not being too hasty; dealing sympathetically and presenting the spiritual aspect of giving; studying adherence to the principles, and using kindness and sanctified common sense; no hard and fast lines excluding the use of discretion; emphasizing the principle that *giving* is a part of *worship;* making an offering at each service; not making frequent changes in policy; discouraging useless expenditures on public occasions. Mr. Doughty wishes especially to emphasize the distinction between men employed and chapels rented by the mission and those employed and rented by the Christians.

QUESTION. Are the Report Blanks satisfactory?

ANSWERS. They are satisfactory on the whole for all the missions; and have been adopted by all but the Scotch Mission.

QUESTION. Do you think the way in which money is used in conducting schools is a hindrance to the cause of self-support and detrimental to the general cause of evangelization?

ANSWERS. *East Japan Pres. Mission :*—Opinions differ. *West Japan Pres. Mission :*—Do not think that it is a hindrance (Curtis). The brethren in Kanazawa think that in many ways such a use of money is detrimental to the cause of evangelization. Mr. Doughty thinks that missions can not conduct schools for less than the Japanese. Teachers must be paid enough to make them feel contented. *Southern Pres. Mission :*— Various opinions held. Some think it does not hinder; some are doubtful; others say, Not detrimental if properly used. *Cumberland Pres. Mission :*— If the question refers to the support of students in schools who expect to be employed by the mission, Yes ; if the money is spent for the equipment and sustaining of mission schools, No. *North Japan Reformed Mission :*—Reducing the salaries of teachers would seem to make it more difficult to retain men capable of receiving increased salaries in other schools or in business pursuits (J. H. Ballagh). Miss Deyo thinks that relatively high salaries paid to school teachers tends to degrade the evangelistic work as being a place for the incompetent and lazy. *South Japan Reformed Mission :*—Mr. Pieters says, Not in the way in which it is used here in Kyushu. Mr. Oltmans thinks it is a hindrance to the cause of self-support. *German Reformed Mission :*—The use of mission funds in schools to raise up a Japanese Christian ministry and make converts is legitimate ; but if used simply to provide a higher education the opinions of earnest missionaries will probably differ. Money used for aiding students may produce both very useful and also very unhappy results. *Womans Union Missionary Society :*—Miss Irvine answers, No ; because only *supported* girls can be claimed to do mission work.

QUESTION. Would it be advisable and possible for the Co-operating Missions and other missions working in the same or contiguous territory to have the same scale of salaries for evangelists and school teachers?

ANSWERS. *East Japan Pres. Mission :*—Opinions differ. *West Japan Pres. Mission :*—Two say, Yes ;

44

one says, No; one, Advisable but not practicable; Mr. Curtis says, Absolutely necessary. *Southern Pres. Mission :*—Advisable. *Cumberland Pres. Mission :*—Desirable, but we doubt its practicability. *North Japan Reformed Mission :*—Advisable and possible for the Co-operating Missions. *South Japan Reformed Mission :*—One thinks it desirable but difficult; one, not possible; and one, theoretically simple but practically not feasible. *German Reformed Mission :*—It would be a great convenience; and there seems to be no reason why such a uniform scale of salaries could not be drawn up and then improved upon from time to time as experience demanded.

This concludes the answers to the questions· sent out. Your committee would in conclusion make the following suggestions :

1. That the question relating to the use of money in mission schools receive special consideration at this meeting of the Council.

2. That a Committee consisting of one member from each of the Co-operating Missions be appointed to draw up and present to this Council for its consideration a schedule of salaries to be recommended to all the missions, first for evangelists and secondly for school teachers.

3. That, inasmuch as two views exist as to the interpretation of the wording of the resolution of last year regarding co-operation,* a committee of seven, representing the seven co-operating missions, be appointed to report an interpretation of the words, " the missions direct their own educational, evangelistic and other missionary operations."

4. As your committee has learned that the " Nevius Plan " has been translated into Japanese, the attention of the Council is hereby called to the fact.

* See foot note page 22.

45

5. Your committee would finally state it as its opinion that the results of the plan of self-support adopted last year by the Council are sufficiently encouraging, as shown by the different reports, to continue united effort along the same lines. It would therefore suggest that a Committee on Self-support, similar to the one of last year, be appointed by this Council.

The following action was taken by the Council :—

1. A committee, consisting of Messrs. J. W. Moore, Harris and Noss, was appointed to consider the subject of money used in mission schools and to report to the Council at its next annual meeting.

2. · To this same committee was referred the matter of a uniform scale of salaries for evangelists in mission employ.

3. A report from the committee on the interpretation of the words, "the missions direct their own educational, evangelistic and other missionary operations," having been fully discussed, the subject was laid upon the table.

4. In regard to the " Nevius Plan " the following resolution was adopted :—As the " Nevius Plan " has been translated and is to be published in Japanese, attention is hereby drawn to the fact ; and the Council recommends to the missions composing it that the circulation of the book among the Japanese Christians be encouraged as a contribution to the information at hand on the general subject of self-support.

5. The committee on self-support of last year was re-appointed with the substitution of the name of W. Y. Jones for that of G. W. Fulton now absent on furlough.

Sunday
School Literature.
The report on Sunday School Literature was presented by the Rev. E. Rothesay Miller, and was adopted with the recommendation that members of the Council endeavor as far as possible to introduce

the publications of the Joint Committee into the Sunday Schools of the Church. The report was as follows* :—

In accordance with the report presented to the last Council, the Scripture Lessons in the *Seikei Kwatei* from July 1897 to the end of June 1898 have been on the Acts and the Epistles ; the issues being just six months behind those of the International Sunday School Lessons. The plan of the lessons has been the same as that of the first six months of 1897, excepting that, towards the end of the year, there were added a few sermon hints. According to the resolution of the Council, the price was reduced to sixty *sen*. The number printed has continued to be 500, although the subscriptions have been only something over 300 ; it being thought that the numbers unsubscribed for could be bound and sold hereafter.

As desired by the Council, a leaflet to the Lessons was issued from the beginning of January. This contains the Golden Text, the subject of the lesson, the Bible story told in very simple language, and a few simple questions, which a child could answer on reading over the leaflet. A little over 2000 of these were subscribed for, and the price was made as low as possible ; one *yen* for ten copies for a year, that is, for 520 leaflets—a trifle less than cost.

In accordance with the liberty granted me to appoint others to assist in the publication of the Lessons, in April I made an arrangement with the

* For the sake of completeness the following extract from the Proceedings of the Council of 1897 is inserted.

In July 1895 the Council appointed a Committee on Christian Literature. One of the functions of this committee was " the preparation and publication of Sunday School literature, the committee co-operating with the committee which had been appointed by the Synod for this purpose." As the final outcome of the conference of these two committees, the Rev. E. R. Miller was requested to take charge of the issuing of a series of Sunday School Lessons for teachers, following the schedule of the International Sunday School Lessons.

Rev. Mr. Hoy of the German Reformed Mission in Sendai, by which he kindly consented to assume the entire business management of the magazine. This relieved me of much of the labor; but, it soon became apparent that I should not be able to carry on the Lessons beyond the month of June, my physician having imperatively prescribed complete rest. In consequence of this, the Rev. Messrs. Landis and Mac Nair kindly agreed to take over the Lessons from the month of July, and to carry them on until the Council should meet and make provision for their further continuance.

Cooperation with the Methodists. It will be remembered that I was requested by the Council to see whether steps could be taken to have the Methodist Mission co-operate with us in getting out Sunday School Lessons. Accordingly in June last an informal conference was held between our committee, and the committee of the Methodist Mission on Sunday School Literature. At this meeting we inquired as to their willingness to unite in such a work; and subsequently their committee met and appointed representatives to present their views to us. The only *sina qua non* with them was that the Lessons should be up to date; that is, issued at the same time as those of the International Sunday School Lessons. After full consideration of the subject, Mr. Landis and Mr. Johnson were appointed a sub-committee to draw up a plan for submission to the general committee, and then to be presented to the Annual Conference of the Methodist Church and to this Council.

PLAN.*

Proposed Plan of Co-operation in Sunday School Publications between the Publishing Committees of

* It is expected that this plan will be in full operation from Jan. 1st. 1899. In the mean time the *Seikei Kwakai* will be issued in an abridged form, and its subscribers supplied with copies of the Methodist Quarterlies. Those who desire to avail themselves of the picture rolls and other helps from America can do so by holding the lessons now issued in reserve for three or six months.

the Methodist Episcopal Church in Japan and of the Council of Missions Co operating with the Church of Christ in Japan.

A.

THE GENERAL SCHEME OF CO-OPERATION.

I. There shall be a Joint Board of Management, which shall also act as an Editorial Staff.

II. This Board (or Staff) shall be composed of three members from the Missionary body of the Methodist Episcopal Church, and three members from the Missions Co-operating with the Church of Christ in Japan.

III. These sections shall be known respectively as the Methodist and Presbyterian Groups.*

IV. The members of each Group of the Board shall be elected by the Committee of Publications of each body. The term of membership shall be two years. The election shall take place at least six months before the date for which the Sunday School work is to be prepared. In default of the election of either Group the old Group shall continue to serve until such election.

V. The Board shall hold stated quarterly meetings at the beginning of each quarter. Special meetings shall be held at the request of any two members.

VI. The International Sunday School Lessons, with the International date, shall be used.

---

* The Presbyterian Group will be composed of Mr. Landis, Dr. Wyckoff, and Mr. Scudder; the Methodist Group, of Dr. J. G. Cleveland (with Mr. B. Chappel as alternate), Mr. D. S. Spencer and Mr H. B. Johnson.

B.

THE WORK.

I. Scheme of Lesson Helps.

1. There shall be three grades of Lesson Helps.

a. A TEACHERS JOURNAL for teachers and helpers generally—to be issued monthly, something on the plan of the *Scikei Kwatei* hitherto published by Mr. Miller for the Church of Christ in Japan. This shall be divided into departments, with editors assigned by the Board from its own members, each of whom shall be responsible for his own department—the departments to be as follows:

(*a*). Lesson Context and Critical Notes.
(*b*). Topical Subjects: as Persons, Places, Customs, ect.
(*c*). Personal Applications and Illustrations.
(*d*). Teaching Hints, with Questions and Answers.

b. A QUARTERLY for Advanced and Intermediate pupils, similar to the present Methodist Quarterly, but somewhat simplified. This to contain:

(*a*). Pictures, Maps, ect.
(*b*). A Simple Exposition of the Lesson, with practical applications.
(*c*). Suggestive Question Hints to aid in the study of the lesson.
(*d*). Daily Scripture Readings.

c. A LEAFLET for the Primary Department, like the Leaflets of the Methodist Episcopal Church, or the *Scikei Hagami* published by Mr. Miller, to be issued monthly or quarterly, in leaves detached weekly. This is to contain the Golden Text, the Subject of the Lesson, the Lesson Story in simple

50

words in *kana*, with an easy application at the end, and a few simple questions all of which can be answered from the Lesson itself.

II. Apportionment of the Work.

1. The work shall be assigned to the Denominational Groups, on the following basis, subject to amendment from time to time by a two-thirds' vote of the Board.

Group I.	Group II.
a. JOURNAL.	*a*. JOURNAL.
(*a*). Context and Critical Notes.	(*b*). Exposition and Application.
(*d*). Teaching Hints and Illustrations.	(*c*). Question Hints, ect.
c. LEAFLET.	*b*. LESSON QUARTERLY.

2. The work under the Groups shall alternate year by year; but with the unanimous consent of the Board such alternation may remain in abeyance for one year only.

III. Peloubet's or Hurlbut's Notes, either or both, shall be accepted as a basis for all exposition, freedom being given to editors to vary by addition or omission as may seem best.

IV. All discussion of denominational differences shall be avoided.

C.

BUSINESS DETAILS.

I. Publication and Translation.

51

1. The Methodist Publishing House shall be the publishers of the above Helps, provided that this Article shall be subject to amendment as provided below.

2. All business matters connected with the publication, including the employment of a translator, shall be in charge of the above Publishing House, the translator to be approved by the Joint Board of Management.

II. Finances.

1. The prices of the Publications shall be as follows:

    a. Teachers Journal ... 40 *sen* per year.
    b. Quarterly ... ... 20 *sen* ,, ,,
    c. Leaflet ... ... 10 *sen* ,, ,,

2. Subsidy. All deficits shall be distributed among the cooperating missions on the basis of the number of missionaries (men) connected with them.

D.

MISCELLANEOUS MATTERS.

I. Overtures are to be made to other Methodist Bodies.

II. If the above plan be approved, work shall commence so that co-operation may begin in part at least by August 1st, and regularly by October 1st, 1898.

III. The first two years shall be considered as a trial; and at any time thereafter either party shall have the privilege of withdrawal, six months' notice in writing being given to the Joint Board of Management.

E.

AMENDMENTS.

The above Articles may be amended by a two-thirds' vote of the Publishing Committees of the respective cooperating missions.

The above Plan has been adopted without modification by the Methodist Annual Conference, and it is now submitted to the Council. It will be seen that the Publishing Committee of the Council will have more power than has been heretofore contemplated, and for this reason it may be well to make it a strong representative body.

I am happy to have been instrumental in starting for the Council a Sunday-school magazine on the International Sunday School Lessons, although well aware of the many imperfections of the work as it has been carried on under my care for the last eighteen months ; and I am more than happy, at this time, to leave it in such a condition that, by uniting with our Methodist brethren, the work will be on a more permanent basis than could possibly be the case when depending on the labors of one man.

The Treasurer of the Council presented his annual report. It was referred to an Auditing Committee ; and, on the approval of the committee, adopted. *Treasurer's Report.*

The committee appointed to present the subject of the teaching of the Scriptures submitted its report. The following is an outline of the report as adopted. *Teaching of the Scriptures and Creed of the Church.*

The importance of careful, conscientious, and systematic teaching of the Scriptures can not be over estimated. This conviction is growing both among missionaries and in the Japanese Church. During the past few years Bible conferences of various

53

kinds have been held, and Bible correspondence has been carried on, with evident profit. These and other like methods should be employed with all diligence. Particular importance should be attached to a knowledge of the whole Bible. Hitherto the tendency has been to emphasize the New Testament to the undervaluing of the Old. The truth should be taught that a knowledge of the Old Testament is indispensable to a right knowledge of the New; and that both alike contain the word of God, which is our only infallible rule of faith and practice. The Scriptures should be taught historically, doctrinally, and spiritually. And inasmuch as the work of a minister of the Word is to preach the Word, evangelists should not be encouraged to give their time to secular teaching.

In addition to a direct knowledge of the Scriptures it is of great importance that members of the Church be familiar with a Confession of Faith containing the fundamental truths of Christianity; and since we are laboring in connection with the Church of Christ in Japan, we should endeavor carefully to teach the Creed of that Church, both in its letter and its spirit, together with the Lord's Prayer and the Ten Commandments.

A resolution was also adopted appointing a committee to report to the next meeting of the Council on the methods now in use among the different missions for the promotion of a knowledge of the Bible and of the results attained thereby. The following committee was appointed: The Rev. J. B. Porter, Mrs. G. P. Pierson and Miss M. Deyo.

General Missionary Conference in 1900. The committee appointed to report with reference to the holding of a General Missionary Conference of Evangelical Protestant Missions in Japan in the year 1900, presented its report. The following (apart from the resolutions) is an outline of the report which was adopted.

54

There are many reasons in favor of holding such a conference. While the different evangelical missions in Japan are all laboring for one great end, to a greater or less degree their methods vary ; and a comparison of methods can not but be beneficial; the experience of one is often the best guide for another. It is reasonable to hope that such a conference would prove a source of much spiritual profit to those attending it. The year 1900 is a century mile stone ; and the fitness of selecting it has been made an occasion for holding such conferences in both China and America. · The fact that no general conference has been held in Japan since the year 1883 is another good reason for the proposal. The committee therefore recommends the adoption of the following resolutions :—

1. That this Council of Missions deems it very desirable that a General Conference of the Missionaries of the Evangelical Protestant Missions working in Japan be held in the year 1900, at such a time and place as may be decided upon after consultation with other missions.

2. That the Council appoint a committee of five, whose duty it shall be to communicate to other leading missions in Japan the action of the Council on this subject ; to invite co-operation in the matter of preliminary arrangements ; and to report to the Council at its next session in 1899.

In pursuance of this action the following members of the Council were appointed a Committee on Preliminary Arrangements : Messrs. A. Oltmans, R. E. McAlpine (Sec.), J. B. Hail, Dr. David Thompson, Mr. Snyder and Miss Julia Crosby.

A committee, composed of Dr. Thompson, Messrs. Ballagh, Porter, Hoy, Moore, Hudson, and Mrs. Davidson, Miss Lansing and Miss Crosby, was appointed to prepare resolutions regarding the death of Dr. Ver-

Resolutions regarding Dr. Verbeck.

beck. The committee presented to the Council the following report, which was adopted by a rising vote :—

WHEREAS God in his unsearchable wisdom has, since the last meeting of this Council, been pleased to call from our midst our beloved brother and fellow-worker the Rev. G. F. Verbeck D.D.—

RESOLVED that we submissively bow to the Divine Will as manifested to us in this mysterious Providence ; and, while mourning our loss, thank God for the instructive example and long and fruitful labors of his servant ; and that, admonished as we hereby are of the uncertainty of life, we exhort one another while it is day. That we hereby express our high appreciation of his Christian character, and many valued services rendered to the cause of Christ in Japan. Worthy of special mention among these are his work as an educationalist helping to found the highest institutions of learning in the land ; his work as a theological instructor and translator of the Scriptures, for which his great natural ability and extensive scholarship richly qualified him ; also his work as an evangelist, in doing which he preached the Word to high and low for many years in all parts of this wide land, never hesitating to go at the call of his brethren to hard and difficult fields. In all these long continued labors he ever manifested an excellent spirit averse to all ostentation and display, always exceedingly helpful to younger workers, advising and encouraging them, and according to them full sympathy. Cut down now before old age came upon him, how can we but mourn our loss and that of the whole Church.

RESOLVED that a copy of these resolutions be recorded in the Minutes of the Council and sent, with the expression of our sympathy, to the family of the deceased and to the Board of Missions with which he was connected.

7. MISCELLANEOUS RESOLUTIONS.

The Council requested the Publications Committee to take measures to secure the preparation of commentaries in Japanese upon all the books of the Bible ; and also a tract upon the subject of baptism. *Commentaries and tract on baptism.*

The Council recommended the missions to make earnest efforts to bring about increased and systematic giving on the part of the Japanese Christians ; urging them to make free-will offerings at each service for worship, and to pay to God's work a certain proportion, not less than a tenth of all their increase. *Systematic giving.*

The Church Missionary Society having recommended that October 30th be set apart as a day of special prayer for the revival of the work of Christ in Japan, the Council joined in the recommendation. *Special day of prayer.*

A committee, composed of Messrs. Price, Landis, Hudson, H. K. Miller and E. Rothesay Miller, was appointed to inquire whether questions calling for consideration are likely to arise when the revised treaties go into effect ; and to report the result of their inquiries to the several missions prior to the next meeting of the Council. *Treaty revision and Christianity.*

At the request of the Rev. H. Topping of the Baptist Mission the subject of the education of the children of missionaries was brought to the attention of the Council. A committee, composed of Dr. Alexander and Messrs. Hudson and W. C. Buchanan, was appointed to confer with any similar committees from other missions, with a view to securing competent teaching in English for the children of missionaries in Japan. *Education of the children of missionaries.*

The Rev. J. L. Dearing of the Baptist Mission was invited to address the Council on the subject of the extension of the Barrows Lectureship to Japan. At *Barrows Lectureship* the conclusion of Mr. Dearing's address, a resolution was passed expressive of the pleasure with which the Council had heard him.

Sermon of the President. The Rev. T. M. MacNair was requested to offer a copy of his sermon, preached at the opening of the Council, to the Japan Evangelist and the *Fukuin Shimpo* for publication.

General Report of work of next year. The Rev. W. Y. Jones was appointed to prepare the General Report of the work of next year.

Next meeting of the Council. The next meeting of the Council was appointed to be held at Karuizawa on the fourth Thursday of July 1899, provided that the Synod meet on the third Thursday; and on the third Friday, in case of an earlier meeting of the Synod.

Entertainment Committee. The following Committee on Entertainment was appointed: Messrs. Landis and Haworth, and Miss Shaw.

Officers and Pub. Com. On the recommendation of the Committee on Nominations the following appointments for the ensuing year were made:
President, H. B. Price; Vice President, J. B. Hail; Secretary, Albert Oltmans; Treasurer, J. C. Ballagh. Publications Committee: William Imbrie, E. Rothesay Miller, M. N. Wyckoff, H. B. Price, T. M. Mac Nair, H. M. Landis and S. S. Snyder.

IV.

OUTLINE OF ADDRESSES

DELIVERED

AT THE

MEMORIAL SERVICE.

Address of
Dr.
Thompson.

Dr. Thompson spoke in behalf of the Council. The following is an outline of his address.

'I have been looking for a Bible character whom Dr. Verbeck mostly resembled, and I find such a character in Barnabas. Like Barnabas our brother was of commanding stature, one whom people might look upon as a Jupiter. Like Barnabas he had much sympathy for a fellow-worker, and could see some good in a man who was suspected by others. Like Barnabas he was a *good* man, and full of the Holy Ghost. And, as in the case of Barnabas, through the labors of our brother much people were added to the Lord. In all these things Dr. Verbeck has left us an example : and thus, though he has parted from us, the results of his labors will continue.'

Address of
the Rev.
A. Oltmans.

The Rev. Albert Oltmans spoke in behalf of the Missions of the Reformed (Dutch) Church, with which Dr. Verbeck had been connected during all his stay of thirty-nine years in Japan.

'The speaker was reminded of the words in James 5 : 17. Elias was a man subject to like passions as we are. The grace of God is manifested not only in the fact that men are endowed by him with gifts and powers, but also in the fact that notwithstanding our human limitations we are used by him for his work. As in the case of Elias, there are usually *special* graces that fit persons for *special* work. In Dr. Verbeck these were notably three: Oneness of purpose; sympathy with the people, and humility of spirit. To those who are working for the evangelization of Japan these gifts are all highly important: in fact they are absolutely necessary to any great success." Incidents in the life of Dr. Verbeck were related by Mr. Oltmans illustrative of these gifts.

Address of Dr. Learned. Dr. Learned, of the American Board Mission, spoke in behalf of the other missionary bodies in Japan.

'There were three special reasons for gratitude to God for the work of Dr. Verbeck.

(1). Dr. Verbeck gave all his life service to the work in Japan. It sometimes happens that missionaries labor in the field for a number of years, and then withdraw either from choice or by the force of circumstances. There are great difficulties attaching to remaining in the foreign field when the time comes when a part of the family must return to the home land and the family life must be broken up. Dr. Verbeck was one of those who continue in the field until the end of life. (2). Dr. Verbeck was a man of learning, but he preached in such a simple way that all could understand him; even the women and the children He thus exerted a very wide influence. (3). Dr. Verbeck was one of the translators of the Old Testament. The version of the Psalms in particular was his work. For all these things we have special reasons for thankfulness.'

Address of Dr. Ashmore. At the close of these addresses, Dr. Ashmore of the American Baptist Mission in China added a few words.

Dr. Ashmore 'well remembered the time—thirty-nine years ago—when Dr. and Mrs. Verbeck, then on their way to Japan, stopped at his home. Even at that time the personality of Dr. Verbeck impressed itself upon him. Dr. Verbeck was one of the kind of men that make history and that are remembered gratefully after they are gone.'

V.

ROLL OF THE COUNCIL.

EAST JAPAN MISSION OF THE PRESBYTERIAN
CHURCH IN THE U. S. A. (Northern).

Alexander, Rev. T. T., D.D.* ....Tokyo.
Alexander, Mrs. T. T. (in U. S).................Tokyo.
Ballagh, Mr. J. C.* ....Tokyo.
Ballagh, Mrs. J. C. ....Tokyo.
Imbrie, Rev. William, D.D.* ....Tokyo.
Imbrie, Mrs. William. ....Tokyo.
Landis, Rev. H. M.*.............................Tokyo.
Landis, Mrs. H. M.* ....Tokyo.
MacNair, Rev. T. M.* (in U. S.) ....Tokyo.
MacNair, Mrs. T. M. (in U. S.) ....Tokyo.
McCartee, D. B., M. D. ....Tokyo.
McCartee, Mrs. D. B. ....Tokyo.
Pierson, Rev. G. P.* ....Sapporo.
Pierson, Mrs. G. P.* ....Sapporo.
Thompson, Rev. David, D.D.* ....Tokyo.
Thompson, Mrs. David.* ....Tokyo.

Ballagh, Miss A. P.*...........................Tokyo.
Case, Miss E. W. ....Yokohama.
Davis, Miss A. K. (in U. S.). ....Tokyo.
Gardner, Miss S................................Tokyo.
Leete, Miss I. A.* (in U. S.). ....Tokyo.
McCauley, Mrs. J. K. ....Tokyo.
Milliken, Miss E. P.* ....Tokyo.

* Present at the meeting of the Council in Karuizawa, July 1898.

61

Rose, Miss C. H. ....Otaru.
Smith, Miss S. C. (in U. S.) ....Sapporo.
West, Miss A. B. ....Tokyo.
Youngman, Miss K. M. (in U. S.) ....Tokyo.

WEST JAPAN MISSION OF THE PRESBYTERIAN CHURCH IN THE U. S. A. (Northern).

Ayres, Rev. J. B. ....Yamaguchi.
Aryes, Mrs. J. B. ....Yamaguchi.
Brokaw, Rev. H.* ....Kanazawa.
Brokaw, Mrs. H. ....Kanazawa.
Bryan, Rev. A. V. ....Hiroshima.
Bryan, Mrs. A. V. ....Hiroshima.
Curtis, Rev. F. S. ....Yamaguchi.
Curtis, Mrs. F. S. ....Yamaguchi.
Doughty, Rev. J. W. (in U. S.) ....Hiroshima.
Doughty, Mrs. J. W. (in U. S.)............Hiroshima.
Fulton, Rev. G. W. (in U. S.) ....Fukui.
Fulton, Mrs. G. W. (in U. S.) ....Fukui.
Haworth, Rev. B. C.* ....Osaka.
Haworth, Mrs. B. C. ....Osaka.
Jones, Rev. W. Y.*...............................Kanazawa.
Porter, Rev. J. B.* ....Kyoto.
Porter, Mrs. J. B.*................................Kyoto.
Winn, Rev. T. C. ....Osaka.
Winn, Mrs. T. C. ....Osaka.

Naylor, Mrs. L. N. ....Kanazawa.
Bigelow, Miss G. S. ....Yamaguchi.
Garvin, Miss A. E. ....Osaka.
Haworth, Miss Alice. ....Osaka.
Kelly, Miss M. E.*................................Kyoto.
Palmer, Miss M. M. ....Yamaguchi.
Porter, Miss F. E.* ....Kanazawa.
Settlemeyer, Miss E. ....Osaka.
Shaw, Miss Kate.* ....Kanazawa.
Thompson, Miss S. M. (in U. S.) ....Osaka.

NORTH JAPAN MISSON OF THE REFORMED
(Dutch) CHURCH IN AMERICA.

Ballagh, Rev. J. H.* ....Yokohama.
Ballagh, Mrs. J. H. (in U. S.) ....Yokohama.
Booth, Rev. Eugene S. ....Yokohama.
Booth, Mrs Eugene S. ....Yokohama.
Harris, Rev. Howard.* ....Shinshu.
Harris, Mrs. Howard.* ....Shinshu.
Miller, Rev. E. Rothesay.* .. ..Morioka.
Miller, Mrs E. Rothesay.* ....Morioka.
Scudder, Rev. Frank. S.* ....Nagano.
Scudder, Mrs. Frank S.*.......................Nagano.
Wyckoff, M. N., D. Sc. ....Tokyo.
Wyckoff, Mrs. M. N............................Tokyo.

Brokaw, Miss Mary E. (in U. S.) ....Ueda.
Deyo, Miss Mary.* ....Ueda.
Moulton, Miss Julia. ....Yokohama.
Schenck, Mrs. J. W. ....Nagano.
Thompson, Miss Anne De F. ....Yokohama.
Winn, Miss E.* ....Aomori.

SOUTH JAPAN MISSION OF THE REFORMED
(Dutch) CHURCH IN AMERICA.

Oltmans, Rev. Albert.* ....Saga.
Oltmans, Mrs. Albert. ....Saga.
Peeke, Rev. Harman Van Slyke. ....Kagoshima.
Peeke, Mrs. Harmon Van Slyke. ....Kagoshima.
Pieters, Rev. Albertus. ....Nagasaki.
Pieters, Mrs. Albertus. ....Nagasaki.
Stout, Rev. Henry, D. D. ....Nagasaki.
Stout, Mrs. Henry. ....Nagasaki.

Couch, Miss Sara M. ....Nagasaki.
Lansing, Miss Harriet M.* ....Nagasaki.
Stryker, Miss A. K. ....Nagasaki.

63

MISSION OF THE UNITED PRESBYTERIAN
CHURCH OF SCOTLAND.

Davidson, Rev. Robert Y.* ....Tokyo.
Davidson, Mrs. Robert Y.* ....Tokyo.
Waddell, Rev. Hugh. ....Tokyo.
Waddell, Mrs. Hugh. ....Tokyo.

MISSION OF THE PRESBYTERIAN CHURCH
IN THE U. S. (Southern)

Buchanan, Rev. W. C. ....Nagoya.
Buchanan, Mrs. W. C. ....Nagoya.
Buchanan, Rev. Walter Mc S.* ....Nagoya.
Buchanan, Mrs. Walter Mc S.* ....Nagoya.
Cumming, Rev. C. K. (in U. S) ....Nagoya.
Cumming, Mrs. C. K. (in U. S.) ....Nagoya.
Grinnan, Rev. R. B., D. D. ....Okazaki.
Grinnan, Mrs R. B. ....Okazaki.
Hope, Rev. S. R.* ....Tokushima
Hope, Mrs. S. R. ....Tokushima.
McAlpine, Rev. R. E * ....Kobe.
McAlpine, Mrs. R. E. ....Kobe.
McIlvaine, Rev. W. B. (in U. S.)..................Kochi.
McIlvaine, Mrs. W. B. (in U. S) ....Kochi.
Meyers, Rev. H. W. ....Tokushima.
Meyers, Mrs. H. W. ....Tokushima.
Moore, Rev. J. B.* ....Kochi.
Moore, Mrs. J. B. ....Kochi.
Price, Rev. H. B.* ....Kobe.
Price, Mrs. H. B. ....Kobe.

Dowd, Miss Annie. .... Kochi.
Evans, Miss Sala* ....Kochi.
Houston, Miss Ella.* ....Nagoya.
Moore, Miss Lizzie. ....Nagoya.
Patton, Miss Florence.* ....Tokushima.
Sterling, Miss Charlotte E. ....Kochi.
Wimbish, Miss Lizzie. ....Nagoya.

64

MISSION OF THE REFORMED (GERMAN) CHURCH IN THE U. S.

Gerhardt, Mr. Paul L ....Sendai.
Hoy, Rev. W. C.*................................Sendai.
Hoy, Mrs. W. C. ....Sendai.
Miller, Rev. H. K.* ....Sendai.
Miller, Mrs. H. K.* ....Sendai.
Moore, Rev. J. P., D. D. ....Tokyo.
Moore, Mrs. J. P. ....Tokyo.
Noss, Rev. C ....Sendai.
Schneder, Rev. D. B. ....Sendai.
Snyder, Rev. S. S.* ....Sendai.

Hollowell, Miss M. C.* (in U. S.) ....Sendai.
Rohrbach, Miss Lillie May. ....Sendai.
Zurfluh, Miss Lena* ....Sendai.

MISSION OF THE CUMBERLAND PRESBYTERIAN CHURCH.

Hail, Rev. A. D., D. D. (in U. S.) ....Osaka.
Hail, Mrs. A. D. (in U. S.) ....Osaka.
Hail, Rev. J. B.* ....Wakayama.
Hail, Mrs. J. B. ....Wakayama.
Hudson, Rev. G. G.* ....Osaka.
Hudson, Mrs G. G. ....Osaka.
Van Horne, Rev. G. W. ....Osaka.
Van Horne, Mrs G. W. ....Osaka.

Alexander, Miss S. ....Takatsuki, Settsu.
Drennan, Mrs. A. M. ....Tsu, Ise.
Freeland, Miss Jennie ....Osaka.
Gardner, Miss Ella (in U. S.) ....Osaka.
Leavitt, Miss Julia N. ....Senabe, Kii.
Lyons, Miss N. A. ....Tsu, Ise.
Morgan, Miss May (in U. S.).................
Rezner, Miss Rena (in U. S.) ....

65

WOMANS UNION MISSIONARY SOCIETY.

Crosby, Miss Julia N.* ....Omata, Sashu.
Irvine, Miss Reba L. (in U. S.) ....Yokohama.
Pierson, Mrs L. H. ....Yokohama.
Pratt, Miss S. A. ....Yokohama

www.ingramcontent.com/pod-product-compliance
Lightning Source LLC
Chambersburg PA
CBHW021226260626
47172CB00002B/617